THE GREATEST ADVENTURES IN THE WORLD

ALADDIN
and the
FABULOUS GENIE

TONY BRADMAN & TONY ROSS

ORCHARD BOOKS

ORCHARD BOOKS
96 Leonard Street, London EC2A 4XD
Orchard Books Australia
32/45-51 Huntley Street, Alexandria, NSW 2015
ISBN 1 84362 471 0 (hardback)
ISBN 1 84362 477 X (paperback)
The text was first published in Great Britain in the form of a gift collection called
Swords, Sorcerers and Superheroes with full colour illustrations by Tony Ross, in 2003
This edition first published in hardback in 2004
First paperback publication in 2005
Text © Tony Bradman 2003
Illustrations © Tony Ross 2004
The rights of Tony Bradman to be identified as the author and of Tony Ross
to be identified as the illustrator of this work have been asserted by them
in accordance with the Copyright, Designs and Patents Act, 1988.
A CIP catalogue record for this book is available from the British Library.
1 3 5 7 9 10 8 6 4 2 (hardback)
1 3 5 7 9 10 8 6 4 2 (paperback)
Printed in Great Britain
www.wattspublishing.co.uk

CONTENTS

CHAPTER ONE

UNCLE HASAN

LONG AGO IN CHINA, A CHEEKY young scamp called Aladdin lived with his widowed mother. His father had died when Aladdin was just a small boy, leaving them no money. So Aladdin's mother had to work hard, day and night,

5

sewing, cleaning, taking in washing, doing anything to keep a roof over their heads.

Even so, they never, ever had enough money, and there were often days when they went hungry. And it has to be said that Aladdin didn't do much to help – although he was always happy and smiling. His mother loved her cheeky son, but she worried about Aladdin. She worried about him a lot.

"What's to become of you when I'm dead and in my grave?" she would wail. "If only you'd get a job, and find some way of making yourself a living…"

"Stop nagging, Mother," Aladdin would reply. A job was the last thing he wanted, for heaven's sake. "Er…something will turn up, you wait and see."

And, amazingly enough, something did turn up…or rather, somebody.

One day, Aladdin was in the market square of his home town. He'd had a busy morning playing practical jokes on the traders and helping himself to their wares, when suddenly he felt a tap on his shoulder. He turned round, and there before him was a man wearing a silk turban and an expensive-looking cloak. The man's deep, dark eyes stared straight at Aladdin – but he was smiling.

"Aladdin, at last I've found you!" said the man. "I am your Uncle Hasan, long-lost brother of your poor, dead father, may his soul rest in peace..."

"Uncle?" said a surprised Aladdin. "You don't look like the kind of person who might be part of my family...besides, I didn't know I even had any uncles."

"Ah, that's my fault, I suppose," said Hasan. "I, er…left the country long before you were born…before your father met your mother, in fact. I should have written, kept in touch a bit more. But anyway, I'm here now, so why don't you take me home to meet your mother? She's still alive, isn't she?"

"Er…yes, she is," said Aladdin, a little unsure about Hasan. But then he decided the man seemed genuine enough. Besides, Aladdin was excited by the idea that he might be related to someone who was obviously wealthy.

So Aladdin took Hasan to his house, and introduced him to his mother.

"Uncle?" she said, suspiciously. "Your father never mentioned a brother. Oh, Aladdin, how many times have I told you not to speak to strangers?"

"Oh dear, I can see I'm going to have to work a little harder at persuading you both," said Hasan. He got out a purse fat with coins and held it up in front of them. "I know, why don't we talk over dinner? Here, Aladdin, take some money, go back to the market, buy us plenty of lamb and rice…"

Hasan paid for a sumptuous meal, and
told them about his life while they ate.
He said that he and Aladdin's father had
been very close, but Hasan had wanted to
travel abroad. He thought Aladdin's father
had missed him so much he hadn't spoken
his name again for fear of breaking down
with grief.

Hasan also said he'd done well abroad and was now a rich merchant, but he had always wanted to return to China to be reunited with his brother. He had made some inquiries as soon as he'd arrived – and had almost been overcome with grief himself when he'd discovered that his beloved brother had died.

By the end of the meal, Aladdin's mother was totally convinced, too.

CHAPTER TWO

A SECRET TREASURE CAVE

SUDDENLY, LIFE WAS VERY, VERY
different for Aladdin and his mother.
The next day, their new-found, wealthy
relative bought them more food, and some
expensive clothes, and paid a year's rent on
the house. Then Hasan announced that he

13

would solve their
problems forever by
setting Aladdin up
as a merchant.

"Allah is mighty!"
said Aladdin's mother.
"It's the answer to my prayers!"

"We might as well get started immediately,"
said Hasan. "I'll take you on a trading trip
with me, Aladdin, and show you how to
make some money."

Hasan bought two camels, and he and
Aladdin set off that same morning. Hasan led
the way and Aladdin followed him,

his mother waving goodbye.
"Listen and learn, Aladdin!"
she called out. "And make
sure you behave!"

14

Aladdin rolled his eyes, and waved back without looking round. But he had every intention of doing as his mother said. He was keen to make the most of this opportunity, and was quite nervous – which is why he kept up a stream of cheeky chatter as he and Hasan rode out of the city and into the desert. But Hasan was strangely quiet, which only made Aladdin more anxious.

Eventually they arrived at a lonely place. Hasan dismounted from his camel, and Aladdin did the same. Then Hasan walked around, head down, searching the ground with his eyes while Aladdin waited, confused. After a few moments, Hasan seemed to find what he was looking for, and came over to Aladdin.

"I don't understand, Uncle," said Aladdin. "Why have we stopped here?"

"Be quiet, you impudent young wretch!" Hasan snarled, and gave Aladdin such a hard, vicious clout on the side of the head that the poor boy saw stars.

"Owww! What was that for?" Aladdin yelled, shocked by this change.

"For being so irritating," Hasan hissed. "You've been driving me mad with your idiotic chatter. And it was a warning, too. Actually, I'm delighted to say that I'm not your uncle, you sorry excuse for a human being. But I could definitely be your worst nightmare – if you don't do exactly what I say!"

"Well, who are you then?" said Aladdin, massaging his throbbing ear.

"I am, in fact, a Moorish sorcerer," said Hasan, "and through my dark arts I have discovered the whereabouts of a secret treasure cave. It's here, right beneath our feet." Hasan swept some sand aside, and revealed a square stone slab with a large metal handle in its centre. "I also discovered that only a boy called Aladdin could go into the cave."

"Why does it have to be me?" said Aladdin, puzzled. "Or aren't you a good enough sorcerer to know all the answers?"

"Silence, you vile worm!" Hasan snapped. "That's just the way it happens with magic things. Believe me, I wish it was different. It took a long time to find you, and getting your mother to believe me cost a lot of money. But it will all be worth it in the end…now open that door, and be quick about it!"

Aladdin's mind reeled as he tried
to take in what he had been
hearing. But despite his
confusion – and his
painful ear – he was
still curious…a treasure
cave below his feet?
So he grabbed the
metal handle and
pulled, and the slab
swung open, revealing
a flight of steps leading
down into pitch darkness.
A musty, dusty smell
wafted out, followed by a
couple of squeaking bats.
"Right, down you go," said
Hasan, his eyes gleaming.

"Actually, I'd rather not," Aladdin said. The darkness and the smell and the bats had put him off, and he wasn't so curious now. But Hasan whipped out a dagger and held it to Aladdin's throat.

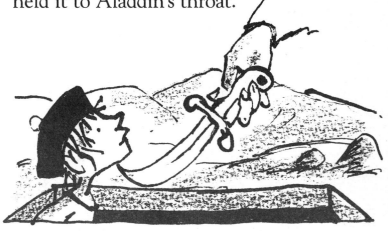

"Er…all right, I'll do it then," Aladdin said.

"Very wise," said Hasan, smiling at him unpleasantly. "All I want is a certain lamp – you'll know which one I mean the instant you see it…"

Aladdin descended the steps, his heart thudding in his chest. At the bottom he found an old torch, and he lit it with a spark from the tinderbox he always carried. He held the torch aloft…and gasped with wonder.

Before him was a huge cavern, the flickering torchlight barely reaching its far side. The light glinted off the heaps of gold and jewels that covered the floor.

There were diamonds and rubies and emeralds and an ocean of gold coins, more treasure than even the Sultan himself could possess.

And in the middle of the cave was a marble plinth bearing a small lamp.

That must be the one, Aladdin thought. He picked it up, and was surprised to see it was an ordinary, old oil lamp, quite tarnished, nothing special at all.

Aladdin shrugged, and started making his way back. He stopped here and there to sift through the heaps of treasure, stuffing his pockets with sapphires and pearls and coins, finding among other things a ring he liked the look of. It bore a huge diamond that glittered beautifully in the torchlight.

Aladdin stared into its strange depths for a moment, then slipped it onto his finger.

Eventually Aladdin was standing at the bottom of the steps once more.

"At last!" Hasan said quietly, staring at the lamp. "Right, up you come."

"No, actually I, er…don't think I will," said Aladdin, fearing what Hasan might do once he had the lamp in his possession. "I'm happy where I am."

Hasan tried being nice. Hasan begged, and pleaded, and wheedled, and threatened, but Aladdin wouldn't move, and there was nothing Hasan could do.

Suddenly it was all too much for Hasan – the long journey, the cheeky chatter, the frustration – he'd had enough of the whole thing. So Hasan lost his temper.

"Very well, stay there!" he roared, and kicked the stone slab shut.

Hasan turned round and stomped away, then climbed on his camel and rode off – and he didn't stop muttering furiously about China and caves and cheeky boys until he arrived back home in Morocco, several months later.

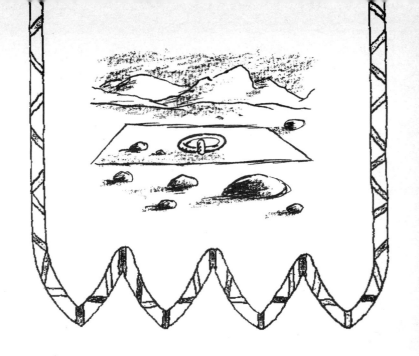

CHAPTER THREE

THE GENIES

BUT ALADDIN WAS STUCK IN the cave. The stone slab was shut fast, and no matter how he heaved and pushed, Aladdin just couldn't shift it. He shouted himself hoarse, but he soon realised he'd been left to die. His torch went out, and he couldn't get it alight again. He sat in the darkness sobbing, calling for his mother, wringing his hands, accidentally rubbing the diamond ring as he did so.

Suddenly a stream of smoke shot out of the ring, strange, glowing, blue smoke that spun itself into a spiral. It whirled and curled and sparkled and gleamed and gradually seemed to grow more solid, until a tall, blue, muscular figure stood before Aladdin, his turbaned head bowed low. Then the figure lifted his head, and Aladdin saw a pair of piercing blue eyes staring at him.

"Whoa!" said Aladdin, scrambling backwards. "Who...what are you?"

"I am the genie of the ring," the figure boomed. "What is your desire, Master?"

Aladdin thought this genie might be telling the truth. After all, he had appeared as if by magic. And then Aladdin realised that he might have been given a way of saving himself from slowly starving to death in the dark.

"All right, then..." he said, and crossed his fingers. "Get me out of here."

There was a bright
blue flash – and Aladdin
found himself outside,
safe and sound, the
genie spiralling back into
the ring. Aladdin was very
relieved! He danced round
happily, then leapt on his camel and rode
home to tell his mother what had
happened. But she didn't believe his wild
story, of an uncle who wasn't an uncle
but a sorcerer, of genies and treasure,
and thought he'd probably just upset
Hasan – and lost his chance of becoming
a rich merchant. Then when Aladdin
showed her the jewels and coins that he'd
stuffed in his pockets, she wailed and said
he must have stolen them from someone.

"And what's that you've got there?" she said crossly, pointing at the lamp.

"Oh, only an old lamp," said Aladdin, idly rubbing it. A stream of smoke shot out of its spout – a strange, glowing, red smoke that spun itself into a spiral. It whirled and curled and sparkled and gleamed and gradually seemed to grow more solid, until a tall, red, muscular figure stood before them, his turbaned head bowed low. But this genie was much bigger than the other.

It raised its huge head, and stared at Aladdin with its piercing red eyes.

"I am the genie of the lamp," the figure boomed. "What is your desire, Master?"

"Wow, another one!" said Aladdin, amazed. "This is getting better all the time! You see, Mother, I was telling the truth!"

"Well, Allah bless my soul!" she said. "You were, too!" And then she fainted.

She came round after a while, and by then, Aladdin had discovered that the genie of the lamp could give them more or less whatever they wanted.

For a while Aladdin just had fun,
ordering the genie to bring them even
more sumptuous meals than the one
Hasan had paid for – the kind of
food the Sultan himself might
eat, and wonderful clothes,
and gorgeous jewels, and
perfumes for his mother.
Then Aladdin paused,
and thought. He would
have to be more careful,
he realised. A sudden
change from poverty to
wealth was bound to attract
attention, and if anyone found
out about his fabulous lamp they
might try to steal it. And that
would be the end of their good fortune.

Aladdin decided to keep the lamp a secret, and use it sparingly.

So he set himself up as a market trader, and then he became a merchant after all, and within a few years, he was the richest man in the city.

CHAPTER FOUR

NEW LAMPS FOR OLD

NOT LONG AFTER THAT, Aladdin married the beautiful Yasmin, daughter of the Sultan. They lived in a marvellous palace and were blissfully happy. Aladdin loved Yasmin, and Yasmin loved her husband, and she thought he was a wonderful man, although there was one odd thing about him. He had an old, tarnished, battered lamp that he kept in a cupboard in their bedroom. He seemed to be very attached to it, too, but would never explain why.

At any rate, things were perfect for the young couple – Yasmin even got on with her mother-in-law, who lived with them in their palace – and that's the way they probably would have stayed. If it hadn't been for Hasan.

The Moorish sorcerer had almost forgotten his experiences in China, but then one day, he decided to check up on what Aladdin was doing. He cast a few magic spells, peered into his crystal ball – and was stunned to see that the cheeky young scamp's fortunes seemed to have changed completely.

"He must have taken the lamp for himself!" Hasan hissed furiously.

Within a few weeks Hasan was back in Aladdin's home town. He knew through his dark arts that the lamp was hidden somewhere secret, and he devised a cunning plan to get his hands on it. He disguised himself as an old man, a seller of lamps, and went to Aladdin's palace one morning when Aladdin was out. "New lamps for old!" Hasan shouted at the gate. "New lamps for old!" Aladdin's mother didn't hear him, but Yasmin did, and remembered that old lamp in the cupboard.

What a nice surprise for Aladdin it would be to find a new lamp in its place, she thought. So she took it out to Hasan at the gate. He gave her a new lamp, then quickly hurried away with the old one.

He knew all about the genie in it, and the power the genie could give him.

"At long last!" Hasan cried as he rubbed the lamp and the genie appeared, with all the usual magical special effects, of course.

"Genie, take me straight back to Morocco," Hasan said. "Oh, and bring Aladdin's palace, too…"

"Your wish is my command, Master," said the genie, and obeyed Hasan's bidding, whirling him and the palace off in a towering cloud of red smoke.

Yasmin was inside it, and so – unluckily for her – was Aladdin's mother.

Aladdin returned later to discover a very nasty surprise – a huge hole where his palace should have been. He was horrified, and worried about his wife and mother, but no one could tell him what had happened.

Aladdin had his suspicions, and remembered that he also had a way of finding out for sure. He had kept a certain diamond ring for just this kind of emergency. He rubbed it, and soon the genie of the ring was standing before him. The genie told Aladdin about Hasan's trick, and how the genie of the lamp had taken the palace – and Yasmin and Aladdin's mother – to Morocco. But the genie of the ring wasn't powerful enough to bring them and the palace back. "Right, then," Aladdin said grimly. "I'll have to sort this out myself."

So Aladdin got the genie of the ring to
take him to Morocco. The genie of the
lamp had dumped Aladdin's palace by the
sea, and Aladdin crept inside, keeping an
eye out for Hasan. But the sorcerer didn't
appear, and Aladdin soon found Yasmin
and his mother. They were very glad to
see him.

"Oh, Aladdin," Yasmin wailed. "You
must save me from that horrible old man.

He says I have to forget about you and agree to be his wife instead..."

But Aladdin was cleverer than Hasan and he quickly came up with a plan to deal with the sorcerer once and for all. Some say he got Yasmin to give Hasan a poisoned drink. Others claim that Aladdin hid behind a curtain, then jumped out on the unsuspecting sorcerer and stabbed him. But the truth is funnier.

 Aladdin told the genie of the ring to shrink Hasan to the size of a mouse, then seal him in a magic bottle with a tiny replica of Aladdin himself. And that's where Hasan is to this day, trapped inside forever, listening to an endless stream of cheeky chatter and jokes, unable to do anything about it. Aladdin found his fabulous lamp, and told the genie to whisk them home in the palace. And that's pretty much the end of the story, except to say that Aladdin and Yasmin had many fine children and lived happily ever after.

Oh, and Aladdin's mother lived for a long time too, and never had to work again, so she was very grateful to her son. Although every once in a while, she would look at him and say, "I still think you should have got a proper job."

But then you can never satisfy some people, can you?

ALADDIN

The Good-for-Nothing Who Comes Good

By Tony Bradman

The story of Aladdin first appeared in *The Thousand and One Nights*, the great collection of Arabic, Persian and Indian folk tales that gave us so many marvellous stories, including those of Ali Baba and *The Voyages of Sinbad the Sailor*. Although the original was put together in the Middle Ages in Baghdad and Cairo, it was translated into French, English and other languages in the eighteenth and nineteenth centuries and continues to be popular the world over today.

Aladdin soon became very popular as a story on its own, particularly with children. It has been told in many different versions – as a picture book, on TV, as a live-action film or an animation. In Britain it's also often made into a pantomime – a musical show put on at Christmas to entertain families.

A major part of its appeal is its fantastic plot, of

course. A poor boy living with his widowed mother, an evil magician, a fabulous genie from a lamp who can grant your every wish – it's great stuff, a terrifically inventive story full of twists and turns and surprises. But right from the start people saw more in it.

Aladdin is a young scamp, a good-for-nothing boy who never does any work and aims to get through life purely on his wits. But boys like that often have a very attractive personality – they're cheeky and funny and love to play tricks. That's why in most versions of the story Aladdin gets all the best lines, and is often seen driving Hasan mad with his chatter and his jokes.

Characters like Aladdin appear in the stories of many cultures. There are 'Tricksters' in African folk-tales, characters who disguise themselves, and tease and play jokes. Native American folk tales have something similar. And in the very English stories about Robin Hood, Robin himself is a real trickster, someone for whom having fun is as important as winning. Aladdin also wins – and through his experiences he learns that it's important to take care of business too. So the good-for-nothing comes good in the end!

ORCHARD MYTHS AND CLASSICS

THE GREATEST ADVENTURES IN THE WORLD

TONY BRADMAN & TONY ROSS

Ali Baba and the Stolen Treasure	1 84362 473 7
Jason and the Voyage to the Edge of the World	1 84362 472 9
Robin Hood and the Silver Arrow	1 84362 474 5
Aladdin and the Fabulous Genie	1 84362 477 X
Arthur and the King's Sword	1 84362 475 3
William Tell and the Apple for Freedom	1 84362 476 1

All priced at £3.99

Orchard Myths and Classics are available from all good bookshops,or can be ordered
direct from the publisher: Orchard Books, PO BOX 29, Douglas IM99 1BQ
Credit card orders please telephone 01624 836000
or fax 01624 837033or visit our Internet site: www.wattspub.co.uk
or e-mail: bookshop@enterprise.net for details.

To order please quote title, author and ISBN
and your full name and address.
Cheques and postal orders should be made payable to 'Bookpost plc.'
Postage and packing is FREE within the UK
(overseas customers should add £1.00 per book).

Prices and availability are subject to change.